For Beth, Iain, Norman, and Sheila
—M. M.

For Tom and Harrison
—A. A.

Text copyright © 2011 by Margaret Mayo
Illustrations copyright © 2011 by Alex Ayliffe

Originally published in Great Britain by Orchard Books, a division of
Hachette Children's Books, in 2011
First published in the United States of America in May 2012
by Walker Publishing Company, Inc., a division of Bloomsbury Publishing, Inc.,
www.bloomsburykids.com

For information about permission to reproduce selections from this book, write to
Permissions, Walker BFYR, 175 Fifth Avenue, New York, New York 10010

Library of Congress Cataloging-in-Publication Data
available upon request
ISBN 978-0-8027-2790-9 (hardcover) • ISBN 978-0-8027-2791-6 (reinforced)

Art created with cut-paper collage; typeset in Johann

Printed in China by WKT Company Limited, Shenzhen, Guangdong
1 3 5 7 9 10 8 6 4 2 (hardcover)
1 3 5 7 9 10 8 6 4 2 (reinforced)

All papers used by Bloomsbury Publishing, Inc., are natural, recyclable products
made from wood grown in well-managed forests. The manufacturing processes
conform to the environmental regulations of the country of origin.

Zoom, Rocket, Zoom!

Margaret Mayo • illustrated by Alex Ayliffe

Walker & Company New York

Mighty rockets

are good at zoom, zoom, zooming,

5 4 3 2 1 and . . .

LIFT OFF! Launching!

whoo-oom!

Up they go, zooming.
Blasting into space.

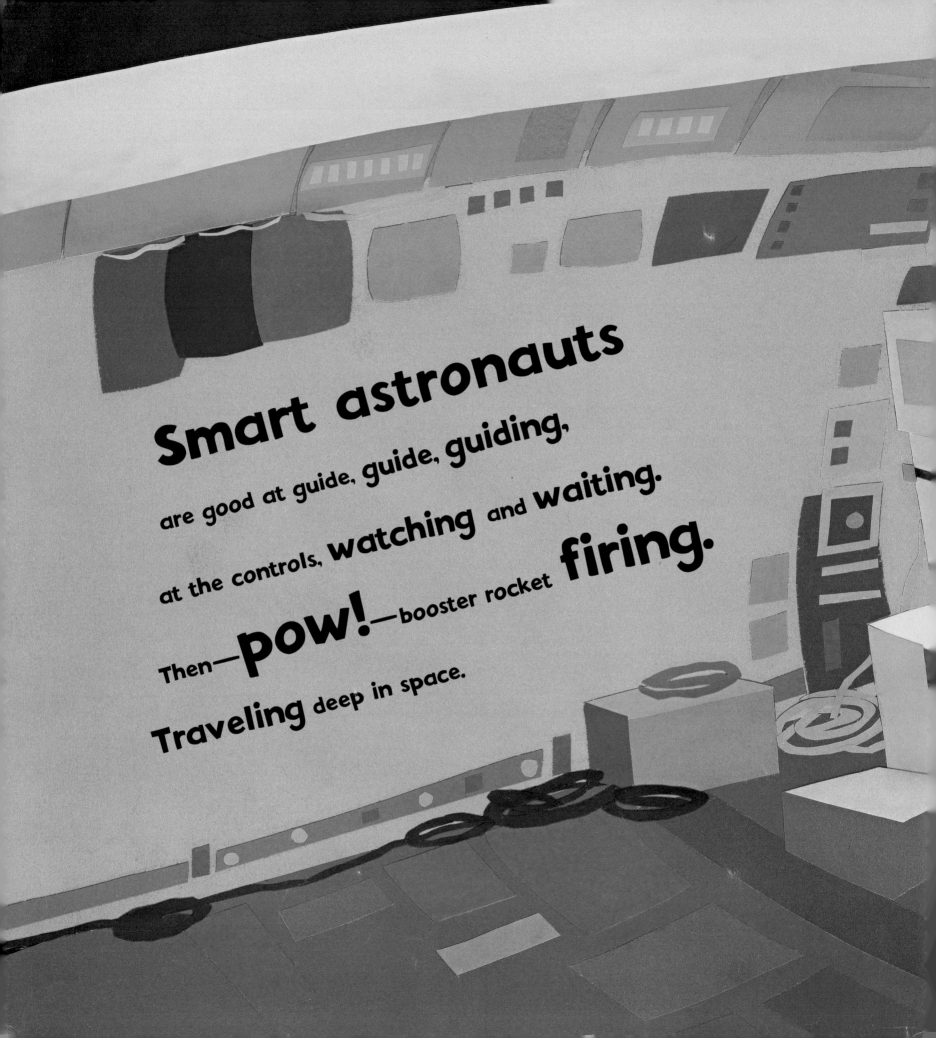

Smart astronauts
are good at guide, guide, guiding,
at the controls, **watching** and **waiting.**
Then—**pow!**—booster rocket **firing.**
Traveling deep in space.

Lunar modules

are good at tricky moon landings.

They leave the spaceship, swooping, descending,

spidery legs ready for—**bam!**—safe landing. Touching down in space.

Excited astronauts are good at moon walking.

Bouncing, bounding... **Oops!** No falling,

Scooping up moon rocks and carefully collecting.

They can work in space.

Moon buggies are good at roll, roll, rolling, round wheels turning, soft dust gripping, across the humpy, lumpy moon . . . bumpety-bumping. **Exploring** up in space.

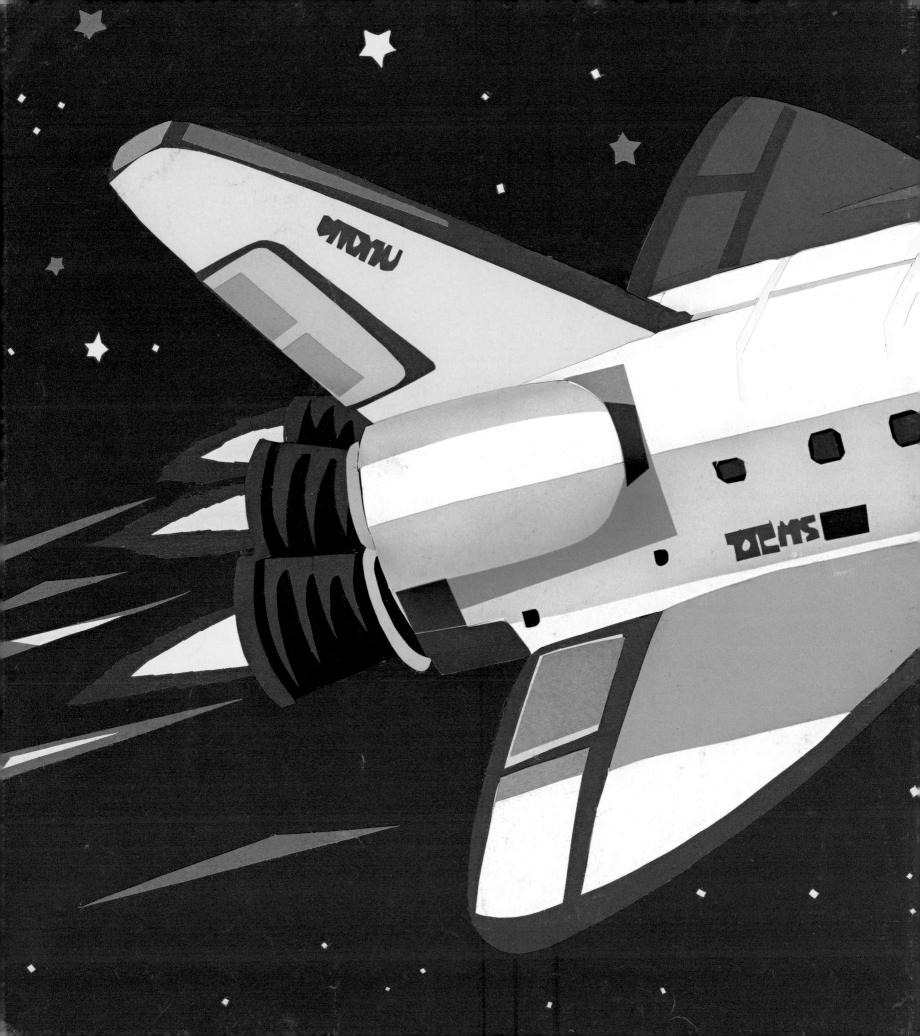

Space shuttles

are good at big-load **moving.**

Up they hurtle . . . booming, **thundering.**

Dock at a space station for fast **unloading.**

Carrying tools in space.

Space stations

are good for **living** and **working.**

A place for **eating, sleeping, studying,**

and—**whoopee!**—weightless

somersaulting.

A home while deep in space.

Bold astronauts

are good at **space walking**,

with arms **waving** . . . almost **dancing**.

On the job,
rebuilding and repairing.
Working hard in space.

Space satellites

are good at around-the-earth **orbiting,**

taking pictures for **weather forecasting,**

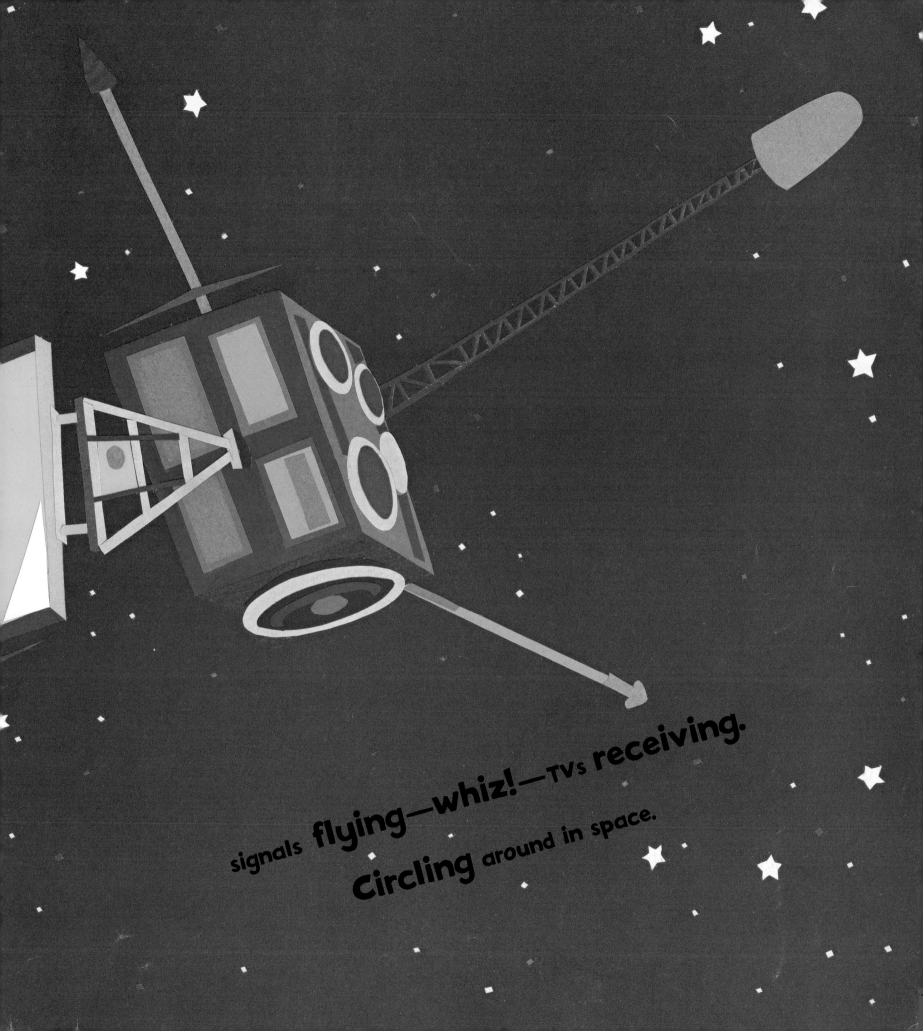

signals **flying—whiz!**—TVs **receiving.**
Circling around in space.

Robot spacecraft

are good at speed, **speed, speeding.**

Powered by the sun, they keep on **flying,**

reaching distant planets and even landing.

whizzing through deep space.

Robot rovers

are good at roam, **roam, roaming.**

They **travel** over Mars, searching, **exploring.**

Wild winds **measuring,** red deserts **finding.**

Discovering in space.

When night has come and the moon **shines** bright,

reflecting back our sun's great light—

explore the stars and **search** the sky,

and **watch** for satellites **gliding** by!